Dear Parent:
Your child's love of reading starts here!

Every child learns to read in a different way and at his or her own speed. Some go back and forth between reading levels and read favorite books again and again. Others read through each level in order. You can help your young reader improve and become more confident by encouraging his or her own interests and abilities. From books your child reads with you to the first books he or she reads alone, there are I Can Read Books for every stage of reading:

SHARED READING
Basic language, word repetition, and whimsical illustrations, ideal for sharing with your emergent reader

BEGINNING READING
Short sentences, familiar words, and simple concepts for children eager to read on their own

READING WITH HELP
Engaging stories, longer sentences, and language play for developing readers

READING ALONE
Complex plots, challenging vocabulary, and high-interest topics for the independent reader

I Can Read Books have introduced children to the joy of reading since 1957. Featuring award-winning authors and illustrators and a fabulous cast of beloved characters, I Can Read Books set the standard for beginning readers.

A lifetime of discovery begins with the magical words "I Can Read!"

Visit www.icanread.com for information
on enriching your child's reading experience.

I Can Read® and I Can Read Book® are trademarks of HarperCollins Publishers.

The Berenstain Bears Blast Off!
Copyright © 2023 by Berenstain Publishing, Inc.
All rights reserved. Printed in the United States of America.
No part of this book may be used or reproduced in any manner whatsoever without written permission except
in the case of brief quotations embodied in critical articles and reviews. For information address HarperCollins
Children's Books, a division of HarperCollins Publishers, 195 Broadway, New York, NY 10007.
www.icanread.com

Library of Congress Control Number: 2022933121
ISBN 978-0-06-302450-2 (trade bdg.) — ISBN 978-0-06-302449-6 (pbk.)

Book design by Rick Farley

23 24 25 26 27 LB 10 9 8 7 6 5 4 3 2 1 ❖ First Edition

I Can Read!

BEGINNING 1 READING

The Berenstain Bears®

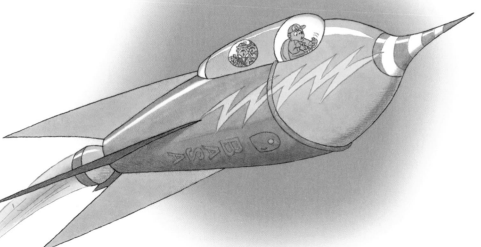

Mike Berenstain

Based on the characters created by
Stan and Jan Berenstain

HARPER

An Imprint of HarperCollinsPublishers

The Bear family is visiting
the Bear Country Space Center.
This is where rockets blast off
into outer space.

A guide gives them a tour.

They visit a launch pad.

"This is where rockets are fueled,"

says the guide.

"Wow!" says Brother. "It's just like

a Space Grizzlies movie!"

"This is the Big Bear Space Rocket,"
says the guide. "It is ready for launch.
We will now go inside the rocket."
"Wow!" says Sister. "It's just like my
Bearbie Goes to the Moon playset!"

The Bear family rides up
to the rocket's door.
The guide takes them in.

Inside are all sorts of knobs and buttons.
"Wow!" says Papa. "It's just like an
old *Bear Trek* TV show!"

"You may look around,"

says the guide.

"But do not touch anything!"

Mama keeps an eye on the cubs.
She does not want them
to touch anything.

Papa looks around.

"There are so many knobs

and buttons!" he says.

He sees one big red button.

"I wonder what this does," says Papa.

He puts his finger on the button.

"No, Papa!" yell Mama and the cubs.

Papa pushes the button.

"Oh no!" says Mama.

There is a big roar!

The whole rocket shakes.

"Who pushed that button?!"

yells the guide.

"I just wanted to see

what it was for," says Papa.

"You've started the rocket!"
says the guide.
"We're blasting off!"
The rocket begins to lift off.
"Wow!" say the cubs.
"We're heading into space!"
"Oh my!" says Mama.

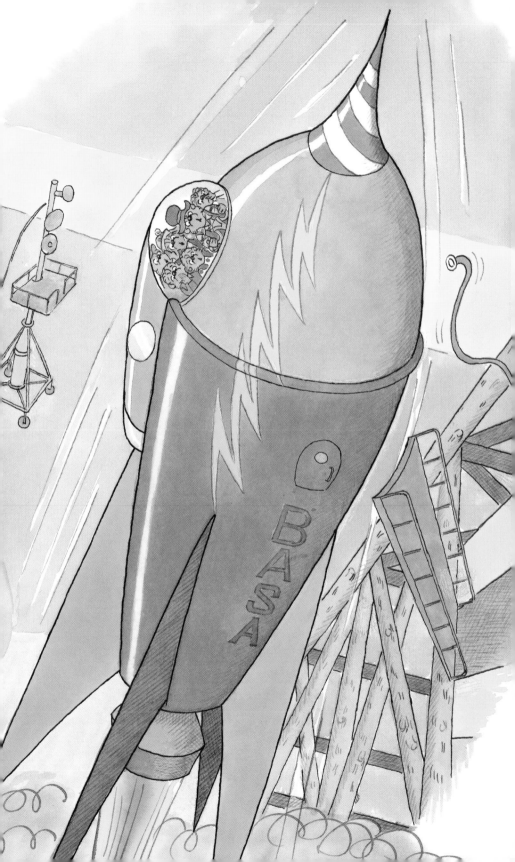

The rocket rises faster and faster.

It goes higher and higher.

The bears look through the window.

They see Earth far below.

"Goodness!" says Mama.

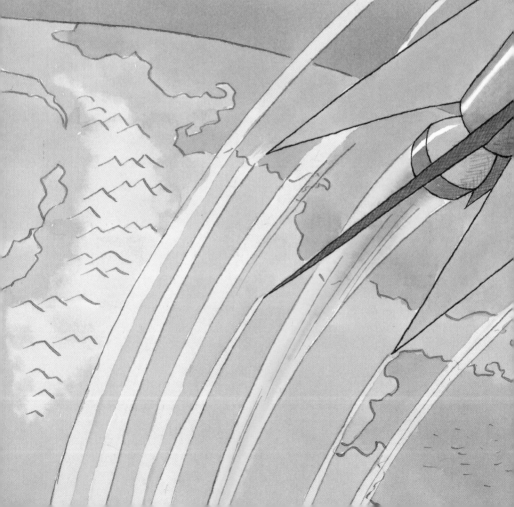

The guide sits in the pilot's chair.

He is a rocket pilot, too.

He takes over the rocket.

He turns it around.

"What a relief!" says Mama.

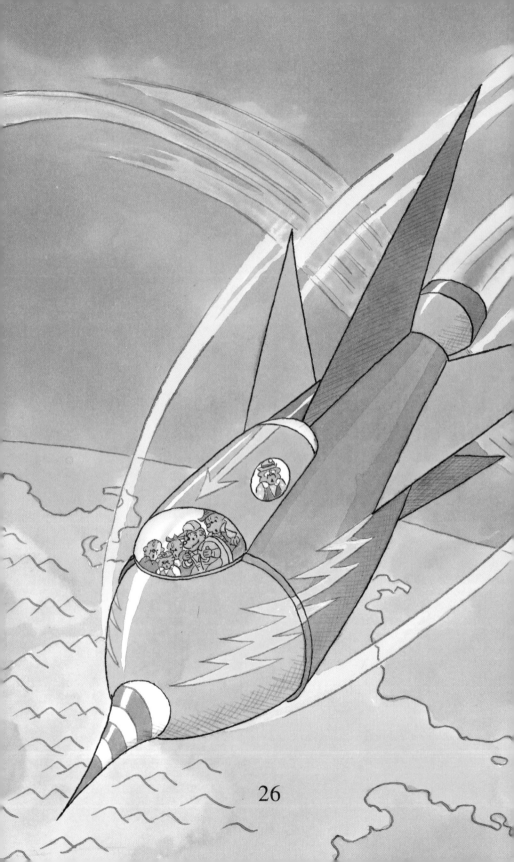

The pilot flies the rocket

back to Earth.

The bears look through the window.

Earth gets closer and closer.

"We're going to land!" say the cubs.

"How nice!" says Mama.

The pilot guides the rocket down
to the Space Center.
He makes a perfect landing.
"Hurray!" yell all the bears.
They clap and cheer for the pilot.

"All's well that ends well!"

says the pilot, looking at Papa.

"I just wanted to see what
the button was for," says Papa.

They all get off the rocket.

Papa gets down and

kisses the ground.

"Earth, sweet Earth!" he says.

"No more space travel for me!"

And the rest of the family agrees.